BC
AB

Other books by Peter Spier

The Fox Went Out On A Chilly Night
London Bridge Is Falling Down!
To Market! To Market!
And So My Garden Grows
The Erie Canal
Gobble, Growl, Grunt
Crash! Bang! Boom!
Fast-Slow, High-Low
The Star-Spangled Banner
Tin Lizzie
Noah's Ark
Oh, Were They Ever Happy!
Bored—Nothing To Do!
The Legend Of New Amsterdam
People
Peter Spier's Village Books
- Bill's Service Station
- Firehouse
- The Toy Shop
- My School
- The Pet Store
- Food Market

Peter Spier's RAIN

Peter Spier's

CHRISTMAS!

Doubleday & Company, Inc., Garden City, New York

Library of Congress Catalog Card Number: 80-2875 ISBN 0-385-131844 Trade ISBN 0-385-131836 Prebound
 Printed in the United States of America First Edition

UNSON
ELEG

37

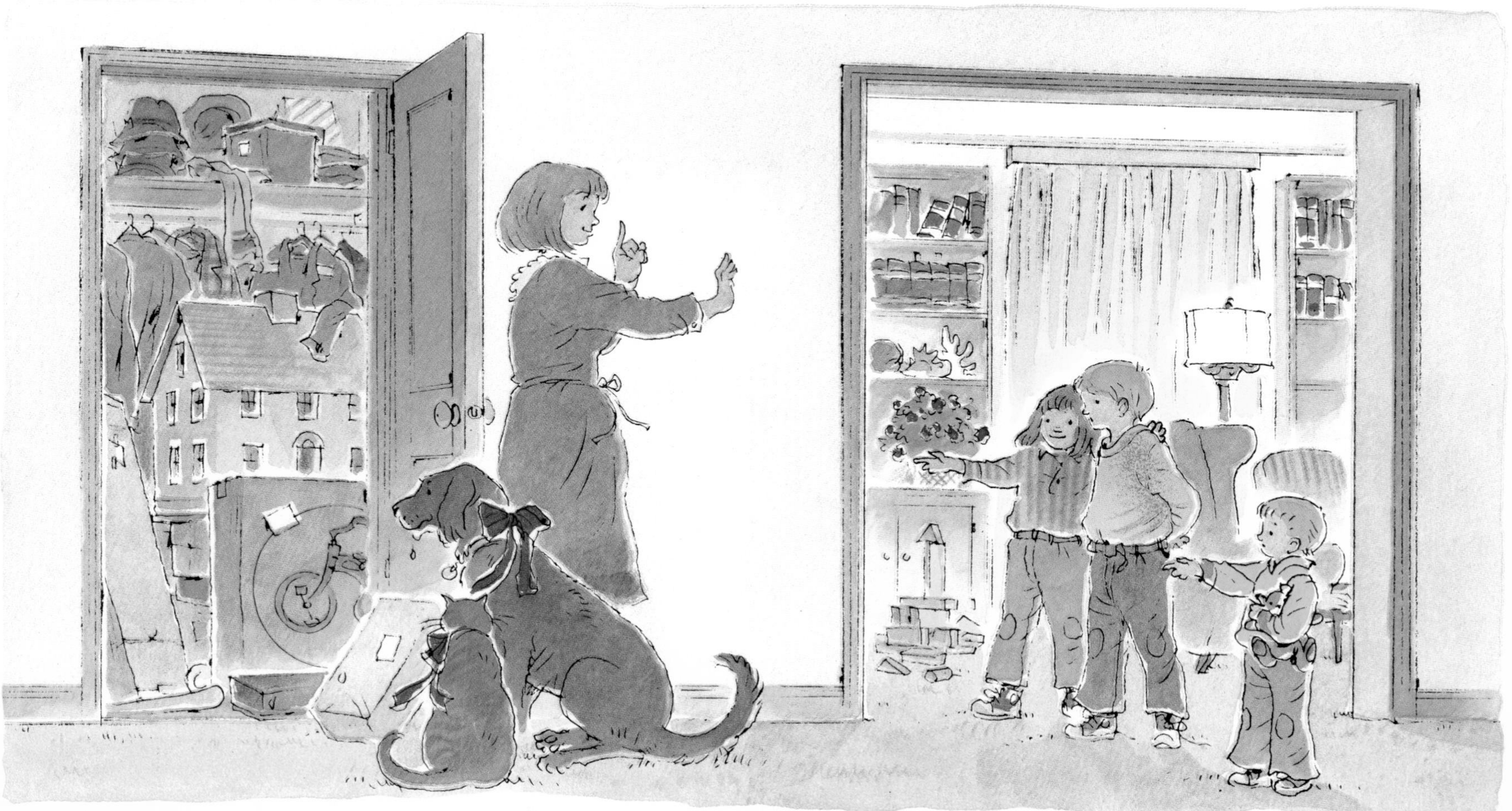

8
9
87
1.40
$.40
GIFT WRAP!
GIFT WRAP!
BOWS · BOWS
Special 3 for 1.10
HERO
Gift Wrapping

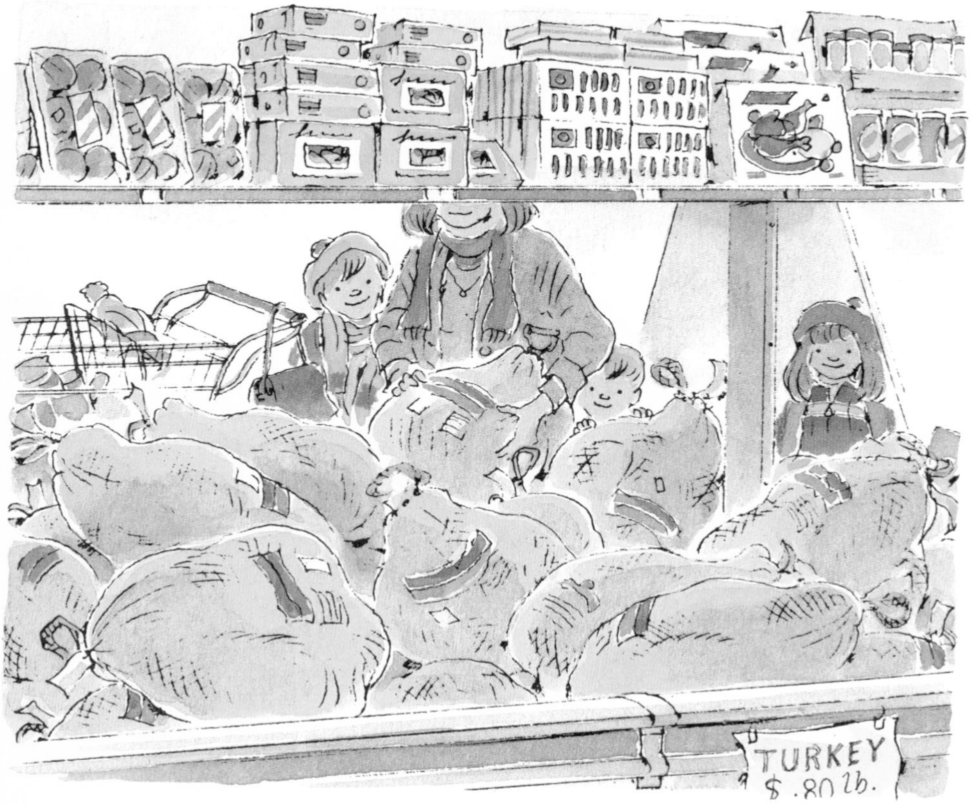
TURKEY
$.80 lb.

3

BAKERY

KERY
FASHIONS

4

NOEL

204
192 197
223

204
192 197
223

S.O.
1806

PARFUM
DE

SALE
ALL CHRISTMAS DECORATIONS AND TREE LIGHTS 50% OFF!

RETURNS

Florist
1883
Radio - TV
SALE
SALE
PLUMB
5&10 Stores
285